Benjamin Cook Taylor

A Discourse

Delivered at the celebration of the two hundredth anniversary of the

Reformed Prot. Dutch Church of Bergen, in New Jersey, on Sabbath

morning, December 2nd, A.D. 1860

Benjamin Cook Taylor

A Discourse

Delivered at the celebration of the two hundredth anniversary of the Reformed Prot. Dutch Church of Bergen, in New Jersey, on Sabbath morning, December 2nd, A.D. 1860

ISBN/EAN: 9783337780746

Printed in Europe, USA, Canada, Australia, Japan

Cover: Foto ©Andreas Hilbeck / pixelio.de

More available books at **www.hansebooks.com**

A DISCOURSE

DELIVERED AT THE CELEBRATION OF THE

TWO HUNDREDTH ANNIVERSARY

OF THE

Reformed Prot. Dutch Church of Bergen,

IN NEW JERSEY,

ON SABBATH MORNING, DECEMBER 2nd, A.D. 1860,

BY BENJAMIN C. TAYLOR, D.D., PASTOR.

With a Manual of the Church.

PUBLISHED BY REQUEST OF CONSISTORY.

1861.

THE TWO HUNDREDTH ANNIVERSARY

OF THE

REF. PROT. DUTCH CHURCH AT BERGEN, N. J.

————◆•••◆————

THIS Church, having been extensively repaired and ele-
gantly refitted, and for about two months closed, was
reöpened for public worship on Sabbath, the 2d day of
December, A. D., 1860. On this occasion the congregation
celebrated their Two HUNDREDTH ANNIVERSARY. The large
edifice, which can comfortably seat eleven hundred persons,
was filled with worshipers. The Morning Exercises were
opened with a Voluntary on the organ, followed by an
appropriate Anthem. The PASTOR of the Church then in-
voked the presence of the Master of the house, and the
Scriptures were read by the Rev. R. D. VAN KLEECK, of
Jersey City. The assembly joined in singing a Hymn
specially adapted and prepared for the occasion. The Sermon was delivered by the Pastor.

After the singing of a Hymn by the Sabbath school of
the Church, numbering over two hundred and sixty children, the Rev. THOMAS DE WITT, D. D., addressed the large
assembly, making most happy allusions to the venerable
men who for nearly the whole of the first century of the
existence of this Church, supplied her with the ordinances
of God's house. He then paid most deserved and beautiful
tributes to the memory of the two deceased Pastors of the
Church, and pointed the assembly to some of the marked
features of her history; after which the Doxology was
sung, and the people were dismissed with the Benediction.

The exercises were somewhat protracted, but there was no flagging in the attention of the hearers, the interest of the occasion being admirably sustained to the close.

In the Evening the house was again filled with attentive and devout worshipers.

The Invocation of God's presence, by the Pastor, was followed by the reading of the Scriptures by Rev. R. B. Camp-field. The Sermon was delivered by Rev. Gustavus Abeel, D. D., of Newark, founded on Psalm 26 : 8, "Lord, I have loved the habitation of thy house and the place where thine honor dwelleth." It was a chaste and appropriate production, doing credit to the head and heart of the preacher.

Then followed a soul-stirring Address from the Rev. Paul D. Van Cleef, of Jersey City, Pastor of the Church of Van Vorst, an off-shoot from this ancient Church. This was a most fitting close to the exercises of the day—a day not soon to be forgotten by the people of Bergen and its vicinity.

There were present on that occasion, and joyfully sharing in the Services, a grand-daughter of the first pastor, and a son and grand-son of the second; also representatives of the Collegiate Church in New York, Dr. De Witt being one of the successors of the pastors of that Church, who constantly watched over the Church of Bergen for a century ; and also representatives of the many Churches constituted in whole or in part of members from this venerable Christian Church. Some of these delegations were large, and the whole scene presented was that of a loving mother greeting and being greeted by her children and her children's children, while all united in lofty thanksgivings to him who sits forever King upon his holy hill of Zion.

SERMON.

"Thou hast brought a vine out of Egypt: thou hast cast out the heathen, and planted it. Thou preparedst room before it, and didst cause it to take deep root, and it filled the land. The hills were covered with the shadow of it, and the boughs thereof were like the goodly cedars. She sent out her boughs unto the sea, and her branches unto the river."

The pious Asaph penned this Psalm on some occasion of the distress of the Israel of God. In it he seeks Divine favor, craving God's presence, while he complains of the rebukes they were receiving, and institutes a comparison between the Church of God and a vine, and a vineyard which had flourished and had seen and felt times of calamity.

The root of this vine is Christ. The branches are God's believing people, and when gathered into a Church state are appropriately represented by the vine and its branches.

This figure as happily sets forth an individual Church as the whole body of the visible Church of God on earth.

Our illustration of the subject shall be drawn from this Christian Church, whose Two Hundredth Anniversary we now celebrate.

She bears the name of "The Reformed Protestant Dutch Church of Bergen, in New Jersey." They who constituted it were descended from those who fearlessly entered their *Protest*, in the sixteenth century, against Papal rule and the unscriptural tenets and practices of the Church of Rome; and the *Reformed* Protestant Dutch, because we are of those who differed from some early Protestants, and from Luther, on some points especially regarding the bodily presence of Christ in the Holy Supper. We are the Reformed Protestant *Dutch* Church, being in the lineal descent from that branch of the Church of the Reformation organized in Holland.

The symbols of her doctrinal faith and polity are primarily from the action of those who met at Antwerp, in 1563, and adopted a system of principles and rules which laid the foundation, and in a great measure formed the full texture of church government and order adopted by subsequent Synods.

After the early settlement of New York, by Hollanders, we find that in 1618 a settlement was made on this western shore of the Hudson or North river. It was, however, a mere trading place with the Indians, and a few plantations were cultivated.

These were abandoned about the close of 1651, and not re-peopled until the latter part of 1660 and early in 1661. Preparatory to this reöccupancy a purchase was made, in 1658, of a tract of land long known as "*Bergen*," conveyed by the Indians to the Lord Director General and Council of New Netherlands; and in 1661 it was by the same Director General and Council, deeded to the then inhabitants of the village of Bergen; thus showing that in 1660 and 1661 the re-peopling of the place occurred. Subsequent documents show that "from the early settlement of the country" this Church existed. It was coëval with the reöccupation of the soil; and one of the certificates of character and church membership bears the date of Nov. 27th, 1660.

A distinguished civil historian mentions the existence of a log church in this place in 1661, the very year in which the inhabitants secured their title to the lands on which they had located.

Two centuries having rolled away since the organization of this Church, we shall take a very succinct retrospect, and hope to derive instruction of large import from some prominent facts in her history. She is "a vine which God brought here, and cast out the heathen and planted it. He prepared room before it and did cause it to take deep root."

It is not intended on this occasion to detail the events of her history, as this has been more fully done in another form,[*] but to endeavor to derive profit from certain principles which she has maintained, and which are developed in her church life.

---

* See Annals of Classis of Bergen.

We shall call attention to some instructions derived from her history.

By it we are taught to love and maintain the doctrines of grace revealed in the Scriptures.

These we recognise in our Confession of Faith, the Canons of the Synod of Dordrecht, the Heidelberg Catechism, and the Liturgy of the Church. They embrace that system of faith which the Reformers valued, and the ablest divines of the centuries subsequent to the Reformation accounted the very best inheritance they could transmit to their children's children, because they believed it to be "the truth as it is in Jesus."

The pious ancestors of this congregation brought with them from Holland their Bibles, the articles of their holy faith, and the evidences of their moral and religious position. In the cultivation of piety they sought instruction only from those who were competent, able ministers of the New Testament. In their settlement here, in a strange land, and using only the language of their mother country, stated pulpit ministrations could not be had. But their covenant God must be worshiped, and we, at this remote period, looking back, see them felling the forest and clearing a beautiful knoll on which to rear a rude structure for the service of God. Think of the first Sabbath's worship on the soil of this goodly State: the congregation small, and probably on that occasion without even an ambassador for Christ to speak unto them the words of life. There they approached the mercy seat in the use of the Liturgy of the Church, as their Clerk, known as "*a help*" in the sanctuary, conducted their devotional exercises; reading God's commandments, the scripture lesson for the day, and some choice discourse from the pen of some faithful herald of the Cross.

Thus beginning, they continued from Sabbath to Sabbath, receiving only occasional ministrations from the living teacher, and the administration of God's ordinances but seldom; yet cheering, and comforting, and establishing them in their most holy faith.

Then a small advance is made, as stated dispensations of the Word and ordinances were covenanted for—but only for *thrice* in a year. In the long lapse of *ninety years or more*, we find them still adhering to this precious faith once delivered to the saints, and waiting for far more of its power and joy.

In the Lord's own time the herald of the Gospel greets them, and the oral testimony of Christ's ambassadors is, almost in unbroken service, sustained down to this sacred hour in which we celebrate their abiding, unfaltering faith as a Church for two hundred years.

They who watched over them for nearly a century were a *noble band*. Henry Selyns, John and Samuel Megapolensis, (father and son), Wilhelmus Van Nieuwenhuysen, Casparus Van Zeuren, and Gualtherus Du Bois, the last of whom thus ministered to them for fifty years, and received his death stroke while in the act of preparation for one more service here. No one of them failed in their pastoral charges to contend earnestly for the faith, holding fast the form of sound words.

However amazing the fact of a Church living and thriving without a pastor for nearly a century, our first thoughts of it are chastened and turned from incredulity to admiration and gratitude for the sovereign grace of God in perpetuating and so blessing this Church, that during that period, when population was sparse, three hundred and eighty individuals were admitted to holy communion.

Think of the untiring watchfulness maintained for the transmission of the faith of God's elect to their posterity, as they provided for themselves and their successors, in a few years after their first rude structure was reared, their substantial stone church in 1680.

This done, they laid by in store for a future ministry, and though many of them died without the sight, they knew the God of Zion lived and would give them a minister for the house of their God.

What though a first attempt proved vain, by a shameful imposture of one who had but a pretender's claim to the gospel ministry? The deception taught them caution, and again they move in the work. They choose a godly youth. He must yet be taught the sound system of theological truth. They send him away across the ocean to be fitted for his work. Four years and more roll round, and *William Jackson* is greeted as an ordained, well instructed servant of God.

They heard his words with gladness. God's ambassador proved an able and acceptable defender of the faith for thirty-two years; when, having led them in ways of righteousness, disease preys upon him, and he is bowed down and broken in body and mind, and can no more give utterance to the truths of the Gospel.

Then followed the earnest, faithful instructions, for thirty-five years, of *John Cornelison*, well instructed and qualified for his work. Ever watchful for the truth and its influence, and ready, when assailed by infidelity or error, to urge it with wholesome, well established argument, so that Christ's Gospel should be held forth in its purity. He sealed his testimony with his latest breath, in the words, " Here, Lord, am I, a poor, helpless sinner, waiting for thee; in full faith founded on thee as the eternal God."

And may not I, who have pleaded here for Jesus for nearly thirty-three years, be permitted at least to say, I have taught you in the fear of God, and endeavored to preach to you Jesus Christ and him crucified? Blessed Master! forgive the imperfection of these ministrations.

Two hundred years of gospel worship! One hundred years of gospel ministrations by only three successive pastors; and the Church holding on to the wholesome doctrines of our Calvinistic faith, unwavering, and we trust with holy profit. Let us stand fast herein evermore. Be firm and contend earnestly, not with friends only, but against foes within or without, seen or unseen.

The history of this Church teaches us to regard the order and government of God's house, both as to worship and discipline.

Call to mind again, her long continued dependence on mere casual and infrequent pulpit services; the lack of the kind attentions of the minister of Christ at the bed of sickness and death; the multitude of those whose closing scenes of life were cheered by no such consolations; yet, guided by the truth of God's Word, cherishing ever the worship and order of his house.

Read it in their faithful abiding by the law of that house. How orderly their arrangements for stated worship and for communion service, (always on *Monday*, because the servant of the Lord could not be spared from his own pulpit on the Sabbath). What though the Sabbath passed? A service of holy communion could, and did, command their presence from far and near. What though, when long and many years had rolled away under a scanty dispensation of God's word, their first attempt was rendered null and void by fearful imposture? How orderly their demeanor! No covenant could be enforced until the ecclesiastical body to which the Church belonged had given her approval; and when the imposition was attested, how quiet was their submission, and how firmly they bade the man depart out of their coasts!

See the same in patient waiting for the holy ordination, by the Classis of Amsterdam, of the youthful Jackson, and the commission for his installation. *Then* their joy abounded by Christ.

This vine dresser cultivated the vineyard of which he was made the keeper. It had lived and borne some fruit; but it was comparatively as the fruit of an uncultivated vine. He watched it, and pruned it, and watered it, as one sent of God. In his early ministry he saw the clusters of fruit, and in 1759, just when closing the first hundred years of its existence, a beautiful vintage is gathered. Twenty souls, at one time, tell of the hope that maketh not ashamed. The heathen had been cast out, the vine had taken deep root, God had prepared room for it, and beauty covered it.

Let us change the figure. You may have heard it said of the century plant, "that day unto day it uttereth speech, night unto night it showeth knowledge."

For years, consecutively, its awkward forms excite curiosity, and when fathers, and children, and children's children, have patiently waited, it fulfills the continued dark prophecies concerning it, and develops the beauties so long concealed within it, proclaiming the grace and power of him "who maketh every thing beautiful in its season."

When, moreover, the stirring scenes of the Revolution in this land, struggling for liberty, were passing, and trials often and varied were experienced, the inhabitants compelled to flee for safety, and the flock scattered, even then the officers of this and other Churches of the Classis of Hackensack made vigorous efforts to ascertain the wants, spiritual and temporal, of the dispersed families; and their reports of these afflictions were transmitted to the higher judicatures for counsel, prayers and relief.

When emerging from the fierce conflicts in the Churches, respecting their ecclesiastical government, as separation from the mother Church in Holland was urged for convenience and profit, this Church was found by her representatives in the Convention, in 1772, which framed the Constitution of the Church which was to govern them in this land.

Then form and consistency were given them, in the proper establishment of the judicatures which, in happy order, are maintaining the peace and urging the prosperity of our Reformed Zion.

Note the order and appropriate action of this Church when her first pastor experienced the stroke from the hand of the all wise God, and was prostrated by disease. With calm composure they await the hour when his retirement should be effected and a reasonable provision be made for his comfort. On this sacred spot, where now we worship, he lived, and loved, and prayed, for his people; and here, twenty-four years after his inability to officiate at God's altar, he yielded up the ghost and went to his reward, gathered to his fathers in a good old age, having passed his four score years. Now, within these walls his memorial tablet is placed by the hands of children and children's children, of those to whom he spake the words of eternal life.

Nor do we find any thing but increasing illustration of the maintenance of order and conformity to well digested rules of government under the blessed pastorate of the successor of Mr. Jackson, (the Rev. John Cornelison), who rigidly sought ever to maintain the law of God's house. For eight years he was in the double charge of this congregation and that of English Neighborhood, and subsequently only here until his death. The whole record of his

ministry is that of the law of the house, of perseve-
rance in duty, of the upholding a pastor's hands and
encouraging his heart, while endeavoring to mete
out righteousness always, yet tenderly but firmly
when discipline was demanded.

We humbly trust the enlarged calls to duty under
the present pastorate, of nearly thirty-three years'
duration, will show that with the same hallowed
purpose, steadfastness has been maintained and Zion
strengthened. Though some diversities of sentiment
have from time to time arisen, and now and then a
few have withdrawn, yet never has this Church
known an open schism. How replete with instruction to us all to maintain, with love and firmness,
the order of God's house.

With what beauty does this rise to view when we
look to the obligations of the Church of God to en-
large the place of her tent, to stretch forth the cur-
tain of her habitation, to break forth on the right
hand and on the left, and to rejoice in her seed in-
heriting the Gentiles; to arise, shine, because her
light is come and the glory of the Lord has risen
uopn her?

Bearing witness unto this are the Churches which
are the branches, and the offshoots again from the
branches. Such are Bergen Neck, Bergen Point,
Jersey City, and Van Voorst, Hoboken, and the
First Presbyterian Church in this place, and, in part,
Keyport, in Monmouth county, and Rocky Hill, in
Somerset county. And yet the original vine is
vigorous, and, we trust, in decorous manner holding
on her way, strengthened and strengthening others,

and to-day celebrating her two hundredth anniversary, with her sons and daughters joyous, as they
enter this house of God, repaired, and appropriately
and tastefully decorated, saying: "How amiable are
thy tabernacles, oh Lord of Hosts," and, in the re-
membrance of the past, "Our fathers, where are
they? and the prophets, do they live forever?"

The history of this Church teaches us the value of
the institutions of learning and religion connected
with this reformed branch of the Church of Christ.
Ever prizing an able ministry, she has recognized
her obligations to see that it is maintained. Her
demand of the youth of her choice as her future
pastor, to go far hence and obtain and use the best
facilities furnished in the mother country, for ac-
quiring mental and holy furniture for his usefulness
in the service of Christ's Church, to which he looked
forward; her honorable provision for aiding him
therein; her patient waiting for him (as written in
his call), "Praying God to take his heart into His
fear, and as far as the Lord please, to take him
safely over the wild element and return him safely;"
and this, "their deed in true faith," tells loudly of
their lofty estimate of an able ministry in Christ's
Gospel. When they saw, in after years, his influence, no regrets could be expressed for what they
had done. When in 1771-72 he, with an honored
elder, sat in the Convention to which we have re-
ferred, and by their votes confirmed the Articles of
Union and subscribed them with their own hands,
one of which covenanted for the establishment of a
Theological Professorship; when we trace the efforts,

at first tardy and very limited, but onward, until the Reformed Dutch Church appoints the First Theological Professor in these United States, and subsequently preparing to give her Theological Seminary a local habitation, the offer of the Academy in Bergen, for the Theological Hall, is made, and though declined, yet in that Academy provision for the elementary preparation of young men for the services of the sanctuary was made, and her own Theological Seminary shared her benefactions, as on a single Sabbath in 1822, she plighted her faith for one thousand dollars, and redeemed the pledge; as one of her sons subsequently bequeathed it two thousand dollars, and even recently some of you now present have strengthened her College with your tuition scholarships and other valuable gifts; as for years her missions have shared your bounty in the domestic and foreign fields, and we have witnessed the progress of our Churches at home and abroad, springing up, and budding, and blossoming, as the rose, we are glad and praise God, that of her it may be said: "She sent out her boughs unto the sea and her branches unto the river." Thus we learn to prize the institutions founded by her fathers, and charge the present generation to teach these things to their children, that they again may rehearse them to the generations following, ever holding fast that which is good.

We are taught the value of Pastoral Ministrations. How infinite the wisdom and love of God, "in that he hath given to some apostles, to some prophets, to some evangelists, and to some pastors and teachers," for the edifying of the body of Christ.

While this Church owes love and gratitude to those holy men, who, in succession, for nearly a century took the oversight of her and counseled her, and guided her ecclesiastical affairs, so that in perilous times she lived and made progress, what does she owe to those who, as their pastors, have spoken unto her sons and daughters, authoritatively, yet lovingly, the counsels of God's word, in Christ's name? Her church life is identified, for a century just closed, with the lives of her pastors.

Full one hundred years of pastoral labor, bestowed by only three of the servants of Christ in the ministry of reconciliation; all of whom were instructed in the Theological institutions of the Church. Under each ministration, the truth as it is in Jesus has been owned of God, to the salvation of sinners, the edification of saints and the prosperity of Zion.

What a company it would be, if all who under the teachings of your pastors have confessed Christ before men in solemn covenant, could come together in one place and be seen by us! How would they recount God's mercies, even the sure mercies of David and his seed for a perpetual generation! What a shout of thanksgiving would go up to heaven from pastors and people, from parents and children, and children's children! What joy would be evinced as they would hail Christ's ambassadors as instruments in God's hands of their conversion, their consolation in sorrow and their prospect of glory! How many also have at these pastors' hands received the consecrated waters of holy baptism, the seal of the Abrahamic and Christian covenant!

How much might be written, did we but know the history and the unpublished consciousness of the thousands of quick and dead who have heard from them the messages of salvation!

When in walking up and down among you as Christ's ambassador, I reflect on a single fact, that already there are several families for whose dead, through *four successive generations*, I have ministered the funeral rites, and that my predecessors did the same, a number of generations rise to view to whom the truths of Christ's Gospel have thus been proclaimed; and all these have been taught to fear God, hate sin, love holiness, and through faith in Christ to walk in the way to heaven.

Nor can we forget the healthful, moral influence of the teachings of Divine truth upon the community at large. Even when iniquity may have abounded, and the love of many waxed cold, she has stood a witness for truth and holiness; God's witness for ages to the inhabitants of this county; but now surrounded in the territory she originally occupied by more than fifty Christian Churches, all organized within the last thirty-three years.

Has it been in vain that for the use of this people, in the generations past, they reared the humble log sanctuary, then, successively, their two substantial churches, and that the present generation have, in erecting this house, imitated the example of their fathers? If God has promised to glorify the house of his glory, to take possession of it, to dwell in it, to record his name there, shall we not value the ministrations of his servants, sent on his mission, to treat with men respecting the salvation of their souls? Then, ever in love, "remember them who have spoken unto you the word of God."

This Church, having existed under the three national Governments of Holland, Great Britain and the United States; having been subordinate to three Classes (or Presbyteries), viz: that of Amsterdam, for one hundred and twelve years; of Hackensack, for twenty-eight years; and that of Bergen, under whose jurisdiction she now is, for sixty years; having had only three pastors, each serving her over thirty years; having owned three parsonages and three sacred burial places for the dead; having under each of her pastors been enriched by outpourings of the Spirit of God; having sent forth her numerous branches, fostered her schools and the College and Theological Seminary of our Church; here, to-day, having with her, enjoying her second century celebration, that happy juvenile band of Sabbath school scholars, and the immediate lineal descendants of her three pastors, and of those who have sat under their holy ministrations, and those who now succeed them as worshiping here—this Church, consecrated with rich and ancient memories gathers together the voices of the past, and echoes them as the present voice of God to his people.

This Church, whose alms deeds began more than a century before this Republic had a name among the nations of the earth, on this goodly hill, as we have reason to believe, struck the first notes of praise to the God of our salvation, and issued the first sound of the trumpet of the Gospel ever uttered on the soil of New Jersey.

In her history century has spoken to century, generation has shown knowledge to generation, God has been her God in covenant, and Christ Jesus her light and her glory, and she stands unharmed amid the heavings and overthrows of nations.

Let these holy reminiscences be uttered from these heights of Zion until the very stones of this edifice (some of which bear the initials of those who laid them, as their memorial in the former sanctuaries, and which we have relaid in this house of God), shall cry out of the wall, and the beam out of the timber shall answer them.

These pews and this pulpit shall proclaim the glory of him whose promise is ever unto his people and their offspring, Yea and Amen.

"For thus saith the Lord, Stand ye in the ways and ask for the old paths, where is the good way, and walk therein, and ye shall find rest for your souls."

> "Two hundred years! two hundred years!
> How much of human power and pride,
> What glorious hopes, what gloomy fears
> Have sunk beneath their noiseless tide!
>
> The red man at his horrid rite,
> Seen by the stars at night's cold noon,
> His bark canoe, its track of light
> Left on the wave beneath the moon;

His dance, his yells, his council fire,
 The altar where his victim lay,
His death song and his funeral pyre,
 That still strong tide hath borne away;

And that pale pilgrim band is gone,
 That on this shore, with trembling trod,
Ready to faint, yet bearing on
 The ark of freedom and of God.

And war that since o'er ocean came,
 And thundered loud from this high hill,
And wrapped its foot in sheets of flame
 To blast that ark — its storm is still.

Chief sachem, sage, bard, heroes, seers,
 That live in story and in song,
Time for the last two hundred years
 Has raised; and shown and swept along.

'T is like a dream when one awakes,
 This vision of the scenes of old;
'T is like the moon, when morning breaks,
 'T is like a tale, round watch fires told.

Then what are we? Then what are we?
 Yes, when two hundred years have rolled
O'er our green graves; our names shall be
 A morning dream — a tale that's told.

God of our fathers, in whose sight
 The thousand years that sweep away
Man, and the traces of his might,
 Are but the break and close of day,

Grant us that love of truth sublime,
  That love of holiness and thee,
That makes thy children, in all time
  To share thine own eternity."— PIERREPONT.

"The Lord our God be with us, as he was with our fathers; let him not leave us nor forsake us." Amen and Amen.

MANUAL

OF

The Ref. Prot. Dutch Church

OF

BERGEN, NEW JERSEY.

———◆••◆———

Published by Order of the Consistory.

CHURCH OFFICERS.

PASTOR.

BENJAMIN C. TAYLOR, D.D,
Installed A.D., 1828.

ELDERS.

JOHN R. ROMAINE

HENRY FITCH

JACOB VAN WINKLE, Junior

JACOB VAN HORNE

CORNELIUS C. VAN REYPEN

GARRET VREELAND

DEACONS.

HENRY LINDSLEY

LEWIS A. BRIGHAM

GARRET BUSH

JACOB VAN WAGENEN

JACOB A. ZABRISKIE

HARRISON PRICE

Treasurer of the Church.

CORNELIUS C. VAN REYPEN

Treasurer of the Deacons' Fund.

HENRY LINDSLEY

Chorister.

WILLIAM SPIER

Organist.

R. C. LOESCH

Sexton.

FREDERICK HONECK

Superintendent of the Sabbath School.

HENRY LINDSLEY

Librarian and Treasurer.

GARRET SIP

STATED SERVICES.

PUBLIC WORSHIP is held every Sabbath Morning at half-past ten o'clock, and Evening at seven o'clock.

Weekly Service in the Lecture Room, Wednesday Evening at half-past seven o'clock.

Tuesday Evening, Prayer Meeting at private houses.

The Sabbath school meets on Sabbath at nine A. M. (Communion Sabbaths excepted).

THE SACRAMENT OF THE LORD'S SUPPER is administered on the fourth Lord's Day in March, June and September, and the third Lord's Day of December.

The Preparatory Service is held on the Saturday before Communion.

The Pastor and Elders meet to receive members, either by profession of faith or by certificate from other Churches, on the Saturday preceding Communion at half-past one P. M., and at such other times as they may appoint.

Persons about to make a profession of their faith are invited to attend to the following, which refers to the "Compendium of the Christian Religion," found in our Hymn Books, immediately after the Heidelberg Catechism :

"When those who are inclined to become members in full Communion of the Church, and to approach the Holy Supper of the Lord, thoroughly know and confess these fundamental truths, they are then to be asked whether they have any doubt in any point concerning the doctrine, to the end that they may be satisfied; and in case any of them should answer in the affirmative, endeavors must be used to convince them from the Scriptures; and if satisfied, they must be asked whether they have experienced the power of the truth in their hearts, and are willing and desirous to be saved by Jesus Christ from their sins; and whether they propose, by the grace of God, to persevere in this doctrine, to forsake the world, and to lead a new and Christian life. Lastly, they are to be asked, whether they will submit themselves to the Christian discipline; which being done, they are to be exhorted to peace, love and concord with all men, and to reconciliation, if there is any variance subsisting between them and their neighbors."

The Baptism of Adults who have never been baptized, takes place on the day of the services preparatory to Communion.

The Baptism of Infants will be performed at any public service of the Church. Seasonable notice must be given to the Pastor, accompanied by the names of parents and child, and the date of its birth, for entry upon the Baptismal Register.

Particular attention is requested to the following, from the Constitution of the Reformed Dutch Church:

"The Sacrament of Baptism shall always be administered

in the Church, or some other place of public worship, and the form adopted for Baptism hitherto in use, shall in every case be retained. In cases, however, of the sickness of the parents, and especially of the infant, it is lawful to administer this sacrament in private. But no private baptism shall be administered without the presence of at least one Elder, who shall accompany the Minister for that purpose; and the same form and solemnity shall be always used as in public Baptism." (Chapter III., Article 1, Section 1).

THE CONSISTORY.

The Constitution provides that "The Elders and Deacons, together with the Minister or Ministers, if any, shall form a Consistory. (Chapter II., Article 2, Section 1).

Section 2. "To the *Elders*, together with the Ministers of the Word, is committed the spiritual government of the Church, while to the *Deacons* belong the obtaining charitable assistance, and the distribution of the same, in the most effectual manner for the relief and comfort of the poor.

When joined together in one Board, the Elders and Deacons have all an equal voice in whatever relates to the temporalities of the Church, to the calling of a minister, or the choice of their own successors; in all of which they are considered as the general and joint representatives of the people; but in admitting members to full communion, in exercising discipline upon those who have erred from the faith, or offended in morals, and in choosing delegates to the Classis, the Elders with the Ministers have alone a voice."

Section 5. "The particular spiritual government of the congregation is committed to the Ministers and Elders. It is, therefore, their duty at all times to be vigilant, to preserve discipline and to promote the peace and the spiritual interest of the congregation. Particularly before the celebration of the Lord's Supper, a faithful and solemn inquiry is to be made by the President, whether, to the knowledge of those present, any member in full communion has departed from the faith, or in walk or conversation behaved unworthy the Christian profession; that such as are guilty may be properly rebuked, admonished, or suspended from the privilege of approaching the Lord's Table, and all offences may be removed out of the Church of Christ."

The Annual Election for Elders and Deacons takes place on Easter Monday, immediately after public service, at which all male communicants are entitled to vote.

THE GREAT CONSISTORY is an *advisory* body, composed of all those who have been Elders or Deacons, whose advice may be sought by the Consistory on any matters of peculiar importance, such as the calling of ministers, building of churches, etc. (Chapter II., Article 2, Section 16).

COLLECTIONS.

Contributions for Religious and Benevolent Objects, including the different Boards of the Reformed Dutch Church, and such other societies as the Consistory may choose.

The apostolic rule of systematic benevolence, 1 Cor. 16 : 2, should be observed: "Upon the first day of the week, let every one of you lay by him in store, as God hath prospered him."

CONTRIBUTIONS FOR RELIGIOUS AND BENEVOLENT OBJECTS.

First Sabbath in every month, for the Board of Foreign Missions of the Reformed Dutch Church.

Third Sabbath in March, June, September and December, for the Board of Domestic Misssions of the Reformed Dutch Church.

Third Sabbath in August, for the Board of Education of the Reformed Dutch Church.

Third Sabbath in April, for the American Tract Society.

Third Sabbath in October, for the Hudson County Bible Society.

Third Sabbath in May and December, for the Sabbath School of this Church.

Third Sabbath in November, for the American and Foreign Christian Union.

Third Sabbath in July, for the Sabbath School Union of the Reformed Dutch Church.

The ordinary collections on the Sabbaths not designated for special objects, are for the assistance of needy members of the Church, to whom distribution is made by the Deacons.

MISCELLANEOUS.

Families are requested to give the Pastor timely notice of removals, sickness, affliction or death, as ignorance of these events may be the cause of apparent neglect on his part.

"It shall be incumbent upon members of the Church, in removing from the bounds of one Church to another, to obtain a certificate of membership and dismission." (Constitution, Chapter II., Article 2, Section 9).

It is recommended to every member, to procure a copy of the Constitution of the Church, and so to become familiar with her doctrines, order and history.

The Pastor earnestly hopes inquirers for the way of salvation will come to him, or make known their feelings to him without reserve and at any time.

MEMBERS IN FULL COMMUNION,

JANUARY 1st, A.D., 1861.

Those who have removed out of the bounds of the congregation, and have not taken certificates of dismission, are marked thus (†).

P denotes received on Profession of faith.

C denotes received on Certificate.

P C denotes the person having first professed faith in this Church, and afterwards dismissed to some other Church, and again received into this Church on Certificate.

The maiden names of married female members are given in parenthesis ( ).

A

Abrahams, Sarah—Jesse D. (Van Reypen).....	P 1854
Ackerman, Hester—John L. (Williams).......	C 1840
Albert........................	P 1841
Helen—Albert, (Van Horne).......	P 1841
Abigail—John N. (Van Dine)......	P 1848
Sophia—John G. (Post)........... P	C 1858
Margaret A.—wid. John J. (Kissam)	P 1859
Aldridge, Joseph......................... P	C 1858
Catharine—Joseph, (Ackerman)...... P	C 1858
Allen, Alletta—Henry, (Prior)...............	P 1845
Ascheman, Martha E.—F. T. (Davis)..........	C 1857

B

Bailey, Mary—wid. Samuel, (Woods).........	† P	1818
Rushton R............................	P	1848
Benedict, Helen—Smith, (Wood)............	P C	1860
Benson, Hannah—Cornelius, (Welsh)...........	P	1854
Bidwell, Harriet A.—Alfred G. ( )......	C	1850
Blauvelt, John G.............................	†P	1836
Bouker, John A............................	P	1853
Sarah E.—John A. (Simmons)........	P	1853
Brigham, Lewis A.........................	P	1858
Elizabeth Ann—Lewis A. (VanWinkle).	P	1853
Sarah—Harry, (Bowman)...........	C	1857
Brinkerhoff, John..........................	P	1835
Hannah—John, (Tice)..........	P	1836
Jane—wid. Henry, (Van Horne)..	P	1838
Jane—wid. Cornelius, (Vreeland).	P	1842
Buck, Cath'ne P.—Ephraim W. M.D.(Ackerman).	P	1858
Buffet, Edward P.—M. D..................	C	1859
Brittin, Abraham	P	1836
Gertrude—Abraham, (Van Cleef).......	P	1836
Jasper P.	P	1836
Adrianna—Jasper P. (Welsh).........	P	1835
Bruchon, Peter Charles.....................	C	1859
Bush, David	P	1842
Eliza—David, (Simmons)..............	P	1818
Garret	P	1842
Hannah—Garret, (Vreeland)...........	P	1853
Julia Annetta.......................	P	1853

C

Cadmus, Eliza—wid. Jasper, (Van Horne).....	C	1850
Carr, Henry J.............................	C	1859
Sarah Elizabeth—Henry J. (Cochrane)....	C	1859

Clendenny, Jane—John V. H. (Van Reypen)..	P 1859
Cochrane, Samuel B........................	C 1860
Collard, Ann—wid. Abraham, (Vreeland)......	P 1818
Connelly, Jane—William, (Fowler)...........	C 1859
Cornelison, Cath'ne M.—wid. Rev. John, (Mesier)	P 1795
Corwin, Hannah M.—James H. (Garretson)....	C 1856
Cowles, Henrietta—Silas H. (Kitchel)........	C 1860

D

Daniels, Rachel S.........................	P 1837
Decker, Hannah Maria—Levi, (Welsh)........	†P 1857
De Mott, George.........................	P 1842
Ellen Ann—George, (Smith)........	P 1840
Margaret—wid. Michael, (Ackerman)	P 1846
George V.........................	P 1842
Georgianna.......................	P 1860
Dillaway, Georgine.........................	P 1857
Ann Elizabeth...................	P 1857
Duryee, Catharine—James, (Brouwer)........	P 1857
John............................	P 1858
Eliza Ann—John, (Van Saun)........	P 1858

E

Earle, Gitty—Nathaniel, (Duryee)...........	P 1842
Margaret—Peter H. (Chapman)........	C 1860
Everett, Robert...........................	†P 1848
Sarah—Robert, (Hughes)...........	†P 1852
Nicholas, C.......................	C 1858
Eliza Ann Euphemia...............	C 1858
Mary Louisa......................	C 1858
Emma............................	C 1858
Matilda..........................	C 1858
Laura............................	C 1858

Everett, Cordelia.:	C 1858
Caroline Augusta..................	C 1858
Emery, William...........................	C 1860
Jane L.—William, (Slack)............	C 1860

F

Fritzche, Margaret—wid. Charles G. ( ).	†C 1852
Fitch, Henry.............................	C 1855
Harriet—Henry, (Morse).............	C 1855
Margaret E.........................	P 1858
Henry, Jr..........................	P 1858

G

Geer, Angie—Seth, (De Graff).............	C 1860
Gemmel, Margaret—William, (Van Winkle)...	P 1857
Gibson, Hugh.............................	†C 1857
Giberson, Jane—Anthony, (Megaw)..........	C 1856
Gilbert, Emma C.—William, (Everett)........	P 1856
Giraud, Elizabeth—Jacob P. (Lines).........	†P 1848
Grames, Marian...........................	†P 1842
Graves, Elizabeth—Amos, (Fitch)...........	C 1855
Caroline...........................	C 1855
Elizabeth........................ P	C 1855
Gravo, Mary Anna—Henry, (Lamars).........	†P 1837
Griffith, Thomas.........................	C 1848
Margaret—Thomas, (Collins).........	P 1856
Gregory, Elizabeth L.....................	C 1860

H

Harrison, Edgar R........................	P 1842
Hart, Sarah—Samuel S. (Tice)............	P 1842
Haulenbeck, Effee—John L. (Romaine).......	P 1858
Havens, Sarah Gertrude—Valentine H. (Brittin)	P 1844

Honeck, Frederick............................	P	1850
Sophia—Frederick, (Flickenscheldt)....	P	1850
Howser, William G.........................	P	1859
Huestis, Sarah..............................	C	1859
Hunt, Alice.................................	C	1841
Emily.................................	C	1841

J

Jackson, Abigail, (Colored) wid..............	P	1835
Jeffers, Moses..............................	†C	1826
Johnson, John, (Colored)....................	P	1842
Abraham...........................	P	1844
Maria—Abraham, (Duryee).........	P	1837
Susan—wid. John, (Colored)........	P	1851
Jones, James N.............................	C	1850
Gertrude—James N. (Van Pelt)........	C	1850
Phebe—John, (Morgan)...............	P	1856
James P.............................	P	1859

K

Kells, Dorcas—James, (Van Horne)..........	P	1844
Catharine—Calvin, (Greenleaf).........	P	1858
Kent, Sarah—Wilson, (Spear)................	†C	1834
Kitchell, James T...........................	C	1860
Knox, George..............................	C	1855
Mary—George, (Edgar)...............	C	1856

L

Lansing, Charlotte B.—David F. (Whipple)....	†C	1849
Layton, Mary A.—Sydney M. (Sherman).......	C	1858
Lewis, Ann—Martin, (Tolen)................	C	1853
Lindsley, Henry............................	C	1857
Jane—Henry, (Hageman)...........	C	1857

Loney, John	†P 1838
Lyon, Gertrude A	†P 1842

M

Mandevelle, Ann—Henry, (Outwater)	P 1818
Mary A	P 1853
Marcellus, Sarah—Rev. Aaron A. (Marcellus)	C 1860
Merritt, Jane—Gilbert, (Earle)	C 1858
Mc Intyre, Arietta P.—James S. (Welsh)	P 1849
Mersereau, Elizabeth—John, (Carr)	P 1818
Midwinter, Giles	P 1854
Sarah—Giles, (Williams)	P 1854
Miller, Elizabeth—Jacob	C 1856
Morey, Sarah—Luther, (Gould)	P 1848
Morse, Margaret—Rev. B. Y. (Oakes)	P 1860
Morton, John W	P 1858

N

Neill, Mary E	†P 1853
Newkirk, George	P 1817
Sarah—George, (Van Derhoef)	P 1817
Rachael—Garret J. (Shepherd)	P 1819
Elizabeth—Jacob, (Brinkerhoff)	P 1835
Henry G	P 1842
Sarah—Henry G. (Van Boskerk)	P 1842
Garret G	P 1842
Jane—Garret G. (Van Riper)	P 1842
Maria—Abm P. (Tallman)	C 1848
Sarah J.—James M. (Vreeland)	C 1842
Jacob	P 1843

O

O' Harra, Rebecca—Calvin, (Scott)	P 1851
Outwater, Eleanor—John G. (Prior)	P 1834
John G	P 1843
Oliver, Eliza Ann—Thomas, (Tuers)	C 1858

P

Parks, Margaret—Merseles M. (Vreeland)......	P	1842
Patterson, John........................	C	1859
Arietta—John, (Bull)............	C	1860
Peer, Ann—John, (Jacobus)................	P	1855
Peters, Eliza—John L. (De Motte)..........	†P	1854
Post, Henry P........................	P	1860
Helen—Henry P. (Mersereau).........	P	1858
Sarah—John, (Van Horne)............ P	C	1840
Helen—John J. (Van Winkle).....	P	1853
Ann—wid John, (Van Wart)...........	P	1836
Cornelius T.........................	P	1858
Abigail—wid. John E. (Prior).	P	1818
Catharine A.—Cornelius T. (Joralemon)..	P	1858
Pond, Eri D............................	C	1860
Adaline—Eri D......................	C	1860
Price, Harrison........................	P	1857
Jane—Harrison, (Barclay)............	C	1857
Pike, Thomas..........................	†P	1838
Alice—Thomas, (Wilson)...............	†C	1838
Prior, Annie..........................	P	1818
Margaret—Andrew, (Tucker)..........	P	1825
Hannah—wid. Nicholas C. (Vreeland)....	P	1846

R

Rapp, Mary—wid. John A. (Van Cleef)........	P	1817
Catharine—Andrew, (Brittin)...........	P	1833
Elizabeth M.—Abm. J. (Welcher).......	P	1842
Hannah—John, (Van Reypen).........	P	1852
Catharine Jane—Andrew A. (Vreeland)....	P	1855
Catharine—Adam, (Van Reypen)........	P	1859
Romaine, John R.......................	P	1842
Ann—John R. (Zabriskie)..........	P	1842

Romaine, Ralph..........................	C 1847
Jemima—Ralph, (Van Horne).......	C 1857
Royle, Thomas............................	P 1860
Russel, Catharine C.—wid. William, (Tallman).	C 1854
Rutzer, Amelia A.—William, (De Motte).......	P 1848
Ryerson, Matilda—John A. (Linderman).......	C 1860

S

Shepherd, Catherine—wid. Geo. (Van Winkle)..	P 1810
Simmons, Mary—wid. John, (Ackerman)......	P 1842
Michael........................	P 1843
Henry P.........................	†P 1858
Catharine—Henry P. (Post)........	†P 1858
Sip, Garret	P 1816
Margaret—Garret, (Newkirk)...........	P 1816
Jane.................................	P 1836
Ann—wid. Peter, (Van Winkle).........	P 1842
Richard..............................	P 1856
Sarah E.—Richard, (Wayland)..........	C 1857
Skidmore, Phebe—Sylvester, (Wood)........	C 1853
Slater, Hugh	P 1849
Eliza—Hugh, (Riker)...............	P 1850
Smith, Rebecca............................	†P 1851
John E..........................	P C 1857
Jane—wid. Joseph, (Pierce)...........	P C 1857
Speer, Abraham...........................	P 1843
Ellen J.—Abraham, (Tharp).........	P 1837
Speir, Louisa—William, (Leggett)..........	C 1856
Stevens, James...........................	C 1856
Ann—James, (Williams)...........	C 1856

T

Tallman, Nancy—wid. Hermanus, (Coleman)..	C 1848
Taylor, Anna R.—Rev. B. C. (Romeyn).......	C 1828

Terhune, Stephen...................... C 1853
        Mary—Stephen, (Joralemon)........ P 1832
        Michael...................... C 1849
        Jane—Michael, (Vreeland)......... C 1849
        Jane—Stephen, (Terhune)......... P C 1857
        Peter N...... .... C 1860
        Anna, Peter N. (Van Iderstyn)...... C 1860
Tice, Nancy—Martin, (Van Riper)........... P 1842
        Jane—wid. Richard, (Van Houten)...... P 1850
        Sarah Catharine.................... P 1858
Tuers, Abraham...................... P 1853
        Hester A.—Abraham, (Van Winkle).... P 1858
Tuttle, Hannah—wid. Joel, (Waldron)........ P 1831
Tulp, Aaltye....................... C 1857
        William....................... C 1851
        Martha B.—William, (Morris).......... C 1851
Toffee, Mary D. R.—George A. (Cook).... ... C 1857

V

Van Alen, Mary G.—J. Pruyn, (Taylor)...... P C 1859
Van Blarcom, Ryer..................... P 1857
Van Buren, Ann—Beekman, (Ackerman).... P C 1860
Van Cleef, Elizabeth—Daniel, (Van der Beck) P 1819
Van Dolsen, Samuel..................... † P 1818
Van Horne, John J..................... P 1818
        Jane—wid. Cornelius J. (Garrabrant) P 1819
        Minedert..................... P 1820
        Cathari'e—wid. Garret, (Garrabrant) P 1824
        John G.... .... P 1824
        Hannah—John G. (Van Riper).... P 1824
        Rebecca—wid. Garret, (Sharpley).. P 1831
        Agnes—Garret, (Van Horne)..... P 1839
        Gertrude—John C. (Ackerman)... P 1841
        Jacob....................... P 1842

Van Horne,	Harriet E.—Jacob, (Outwater)....	P 1842
	Cornelia—John J. (Van Alen).....	C 1843
	John, Jr......................	P 1851
	Mary—John, Jr. (Post)..........	P 1844
	Alletta......................	P 1850
	Garret, I.....................	P 1858
	Mary Jane—Garret, I. (Brittin)...	P 1858
	Sarah—wid. Andrew, (Daniels)....	C 1860
Van Reypen,	Elizabeth....................	P 1818
	Elizab'h—wid. Garret C. (VanWart)	P 1818
	Daniel.......................	P 1823
	Cornelius C....................	P 1836
	Christina—Corns. C. (Van Alen)..	C 1836
	Effie........................	P 1848
	Mary—Cornelius R. (Sickles).....	P 1850
	Catharine V. H...............	P 1855
Van Riper,	Charity—wid. Chris. (Van Houten).	P 1818
	Hannah—wid. Garret C. (Evans)...	†P 1818
Van Vorst,	Cynthia—wid. Garret, (Hennion)...	P 1836
Van Wagenen,	Hartman.....................	P 1823
	Jacob.......................	P 1855
	Jane—Jacob, (Van Boskerck)...	P 1854
Van Wickle,	Elizabeth—John, (Patterson).....	C 1860
Van Winkle,	Jacob D......................	P 1815
	Ann—Jacob D. (Vreeland)......	P 1815
	Margaret—wid. Corn. (Van Riper)	P 1818
	Ann—wid. John G. (Van Winkle)	P 1830
	Sarah—wid. Garret S. (Van Riper).	P 1840
	Jacob.......................	P 1842
	Maria—Jacob, (Sip)............	P 1842
	Gitty........................	P 1844
	Daniel.......................	P 1856
	Effee—Daniel, (Newkirk).........	P 1850
	Alletta Ann..................	P 1856

Van Winkle, Jacob, Jr...................	C	1858
Margaret—Jacob, Jr. (Mandeville)	P C	1858
Maria—wid. Henry E. (Jackson)..	C	1859
Isabel.......................	C	1859
Julia.......................	P	1859
Jacob A.......................	P C	1860
Sarah—Jacob A. (Cadmus)......	P C	1860
Van Zee, Peter......................	P	1856
Adrianna—Peter, (De Kock).........	P	1856
Cornelius.......................	C	1856
Dericka—Cornelius, (De Kock).....	C	1856
Vreeland, Stephen.......................	P	1814
Margaret—Richard, (De Mott)......	P	1816
Nicholas........	P	1817
Betsey—Nicholas, (Van Riper).....	C	1835
Daniel.......................	P	1832
Cornelia—Daniel, (Newkirk)........	P	1818
Abraham.......................	P	1838
Hannah—Abraham, (Van Reypen)..	P	1838
Garret R.......................	P	1840
Nicholas S.......................	P	1842
Ellen J.—Nicholas S. (Van Riper)...	P	1842
Garret.......................	P	1842
Catharine—Garret, (Van Buskirk)...	P	1842
Ann Jane—Michael J. (Vreeland)...	P	1842
Stephen B.......................	P	1850
Fanny.......................	P	1851
Jane—Peter, (Van Horne).........	P	1852
Abraham A.......................	P	1856
Rachael—Abraham A. (Vreeland)...	P	1850
Jacob J.......................	P	1856
Gitty—Jacob J. (Vreeland).........	P	1842
Cornelius A.......................	P	1858
Mary—Cornelius A. (Newkirk)...,..	P	1858
Anna E.......................	P	1858

W

Washburn, Rachael D—wid. C. L. (Tice)......	P 1857
Welsh, Sarah—Henry R. (Mead)............	P 1842
James B..........................	†P 1842
Ellen—James B. (Waldron)..........	†P 1842
Gitty S.—John B. (Vreeland)........	†P 1842
Margaret—Archer G. (Stager).........	P 1844
Abner B.......................	P 1850
Adam R.......................	P 1853
Hannah L......................	†P 1853
Wilson, Sophia—Blakely, (Newkirk)........	P 1850
Wolfe, Phebe A.—Hugh N. (Crane)........	P 1860
Wood, Eliza—Joseph W. (Welsh)..........	P 1857
Woods, Sarah—Walter, (Post)............	P 1845

Z

Zabriskie, Albert......................	P 1836
Catharine—Albert, (Van Reypen)....	P 1835
Lavina—John V. H. (Banta)........	†P 1837
Jacob A.......................	P 1858
Lavina—Jacob' A. (Ackerman).......	P 1853

Whole number of Communicants, January 1st 1861, three hundred and thirty-three. [333].